Dear Parent:
Your child's love of reading starts here!

Every child learns to read in a different way and at his or her own speed. Some go back and forth between reading levels and read favorite books again and again. Others read through each level in order. You can help your young reader improve and become more confident by encouraging his or her own interests and abilities. From books your child reads with you to the first books he or she reads alone, there are I Can Read Books for every stage of reading:

SHARED READING
Basic language, word repetition, and whimsical illustrations, ideal for sharing with your emergent reader

BEGINNING READING
Short sentences, familiar words, and simple concepts for children eager to read on their own

READING WITH HELP
Engaging stories, longer sentences, and language play for developing readers

READING ALONE
Complex plots, challenging vocabulary, and high-interest topics for the independent reader

ADVANCED READING
Short paragraphs, chapters, and exciting themes for the perfect bridge to chapter books

I Can Read Books have introduced children to the joy of reading since 1957. Featuring award-winning authors and illustrators and a fabulous cast of beloved characters, I Can Read Books set the standard for beginning readers.

A lifetime of discovery begins with the magical words **"I Can Read!"**

Visit www.icanread.com for information
on enriching your child's reading experience.

I Can Read!

SHARED
My First
READING

TO THE RESCUE!

BY MERCER MAYER

HarperCollins*Publishers*

For Zeb, our rescuer!

HarperCollins®, ▆®, and I Can Read Book® are trademarks of HarperCollins Publishers.

Library of Congress catalog card number: 2007938294
ISBN 978-0-06-083548-4 (trade bdg.) — ISBN 978-0-06-083547-7 (pbk.)

Typography by Sean Boggs   1 2 3 4 5 6 7 8 9 10   ❖   First Edition

A Big Tuna Trading Company LLC/J. R. Sansevere Book
www.littlecritter.com

Dad goes to the basement.

He has work to do.

I am working, too.

I am working with my tools.

I am tired of working.

I hear my dad walking
up the basement stairs.

He calls me.

He needs my help.

The door is stuck.

I will help.

I twist and turn the doorknob.
I can't open the door.

I say, "I will get keys.

Keys will open the door.

They are hanging in the hall."

I climb up and get them.

There are many keys.

I try them all. Oops!
One breaks off.

"Don't worry, Dad," I say.

"I will call 9-1-1.

Stay there.

I'll be right back."

I dial 9-1-1 on the telephone.
A very nice 9-1-1 lady
answers the phone.

I say, "My dad is locked
in the basement
and can't get out."

The 9-1-1 lady asks me
my telephone number.
I tell her.

She asks what my address is.

I know my address, too.

I tell her.

I tell Dad that help
is on the way.
Suddenly, I am hungry.

I go to the kitchen.

I make a snack to eat

until help arrives.

Soon I hear sirens.

First the police car comes.

Then the fire truck comes.

I see Fireman Joe.

"We have to get my dad
out of the basement.
Follow me," I tell everyone.

I will show them
where to go.

Fireman Joe tells Dad
to stand back.

Fireman Joe takes a big ax.

He breaks down the door.

Hooray! Dad is safe!

Everyone helps take the
broken door outside.

The policemen say good-bye.

The firemen say good-bye.

"Thank you
and good-bye!" I say.

Dad says I am a hero.

I just called 9-1-1.

HMNTX +
        E
MAYER

MAYER, MERCER,
    TO THE RESCUE!

MONTROSE
07/09